RESCUE VEHICLES

KINGFISHER

LONDON & NEW YORK

KINGFISHER
LONDON & NEW YORK

Text copyright © Tony Mitton 1998, 2018, 2020
Illustrations copyright © Ant Parker 1998, 2018, 2020
Designed by Antony Hannant (LittleRedAnt) and Peter Clayman 2020
Cover designed by Peter Clayman 2020
Published in the United States by Kingfisher,
120 Broadway, New York, NY 10271
Kingfisher is an imprint of Macmillan Children's Books, London.
All rights reserved.

Material previously published as Amazing Machines Flashing Fire Engines (1998),
Amazing Machines Awesome Ambulances (2018), and
Amazing Machines Patrolling Police Cars (2018).

Distributed in the U.S. and Canada by Macmillan, 120 Broadway, New York, NY 10271

Library of Congress Cataloguing-in-Publication data has been applied for.

ISBN: 978-0-7534-7573-7

Kingfisher books are available for special promotions and premiums. For details contact:
Special Markets Department, Macmillan, 120 Broadway, New York, NY 10271.

For more information, please visit www.kingfisherbooks.com

Printed in China
9 8 7 6 5 4 3 2 1
1TR/0220/WKT/UG/128MA

CONTENTS

If you've had an accident,
or if you're very sick,
an ambulance assists you.
Its response is very quick.

When the station takes a call
to say that you're in need,
an ambulance will get to you
by driving at great speed.

To clear the road ahead of it,
its siren fills the air.
It tells the other drivers
someone's hurt or needing care.

For extra visibility,
especially at night,
an ambulance on call will flash
its very vivid lights.

To operate an ambulance
there has to be a crew.
They're highly trained. These paramedics
know just what to do.

They carry the equipment
for every situation.
They check to see it's all on board
while waiting at the station.

They store all kinds of bandages,
in case you start to bleed.

To deal with pain and problems,
they've medicine you might need.

There's oxygen to help you breathe,
if you're really sick.

And if you have a broken bone
these splints should do the trick.

For people who are very weak
and cannot move or stand,
the paramedics use a bed on wheels
to lend a hand.

This bed is called a stretcher.
It gives a gentle ride.
And after that it's folded up
and packed away inside.

When the patient's safely in
the ambulance at last
it's time to get them treated
at the hospital—and fast!

The driver travels speedily,
but keeps the vehicle steady.
The hospital is radioed
to have them at the ready.

On the way the paramedics
use their skill and care
to keep the patient comfortable
until arriving there.

Once they're at the hospital
the staff are there to meet them.

They quickly take the patient off
to doctors who will treat them.

Back at base the paramedics
clean and check the stock.

Hooray for awesome ambulances
ready round the clock!

FLASHING
FIRE
ENGINES

Big, bold fire engines, waiting day and night,

ready for a rescue or a blazing fire to fight.

As soon as there's a fire alarm,
the engine starts to roar.

The firefighters jump aboard—
it rumbles out the door.

wee-ooo   wee-o

Watch the engine speeding, on its daring dash.

Hear its siren screaming. See its bright lights flash.

In helmets, fireproof pants and jackets,
boots so big and strong,

the crew are dressed and ready
as the engine zooms along.

When the engine finds the fire,
it quickly pulls up near.

The crew jumps out, unrolls the hose,
and gets out all the gear.

The hose points up nozzle
and shoots a jet of spray.
It squirts right at the blazing flames
and sizzles them away.

The water tank is empty soon,
so where can more be found?
The engine's pump can pull it up
from pipes below the ground.

The fire is hot and roaring.
It makes a lot of smoke.

The firefighters put on masks—
otherwise they'd choke.

The ladder rises upward. It reaches for the sky.
A fire engine's ladder stretches up so very high!

Sometimes there's a platform, right up at the top.
It waits beside the window. Then into it you hop.

At last the fire's extinguished.
The flames are all put out.

plop!

plop!

Lower the ladder. Roll the hose.
"Hurrah!" the fire crew shouts.

Back inside the station,
the crew can take a break.

But the fire engine's ready
and it's waiting wide-awake.

PATROLLING POLICE CARS

Patrolling almost anywhere,
in any neighborhood,

police cars help police keep all things
steady, safe, and good.

To get to an emergency
police cars sometimes need
to be there very quickly,
which means they have to speed.

WOOO

To warn the other traffic
that they're going very fast
their flashing lights and sirens signal,
"Quickly, let me past!"

For giving them instructions
and to tell them where to go
the station contacts officers
by two-way radio.

Some cars have computers
that can use the Internet
to access all the information
that they need to get.

Police cars carry radars
to catch us if we're speeding.
They point them at a car
to get its speed shown as a reading.

When a car is going too fast
police can make it stop.
This car's getting cautioned by
a frowning traffic cop.

Police dogs use their sense of smell
to seek a person out.

This K-9 Unit's used to carry
dogs like this about.

When officers catch criminals
or suspects that they track,
they take them to the station
locked safely in the back.

Some cars have sheets of toughened glass
that firmly stand between
the front seats and the back seats,
to make a safety screen.

Police cars must be sturdy,
like these two that have made

an obstacle to block the road—
a two-car barricade!

Here's a tough push bumper.
When it's put in place
it helps police push heavy things
and clear away a space.

And here's a flexi-spotlight.
It shines a beam of light.
It's great for lighting up a scene—
it's powerful and bright.

Patrol cars have all kinds of things
they need to take around.
Neatly packed inside the trunk—
that's where they'll be found.

They even hold first aid kits,
so if you're hurt or bleeding
an officer can give you
the attention you'll be needing.

So when you see police cars,
as they cruise around,

remember that they're there for you,
to keep you safe and sound.

SPOT-AND-FIND

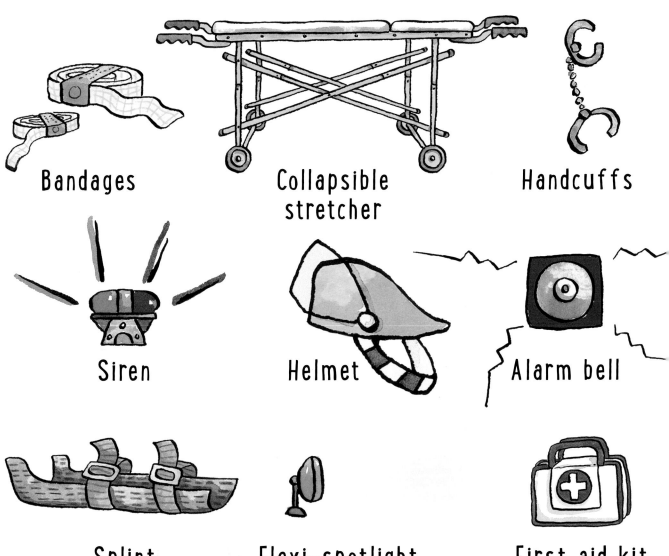

Bandages

Collapsible stretcher

Handcuffs

Siren

Helmet

Alarm bell

Splint

Flexi-spotlight

First aid kit

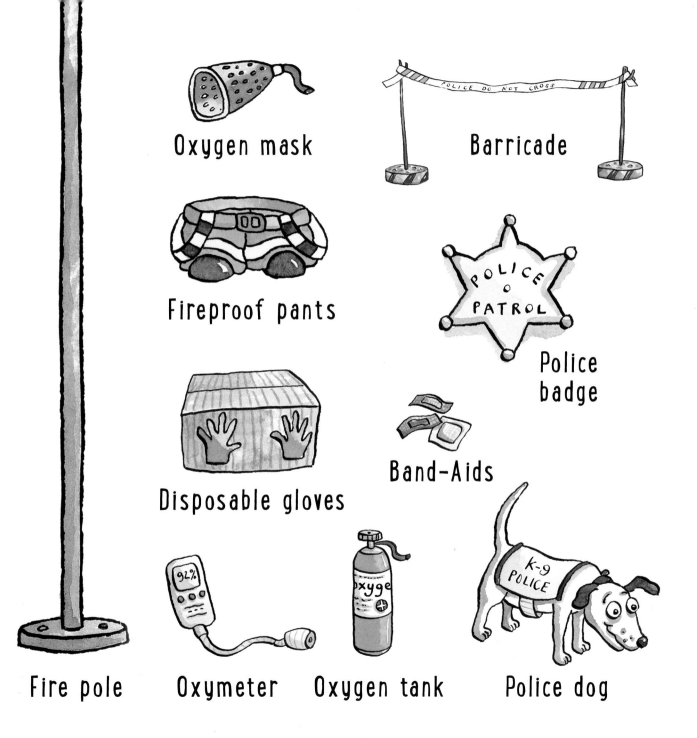

Oxygen mask

Barricade

Fireproof pants

Police badge

Disposable gloves

Band-Aids

Fire pole

Oxymeter

Oxygen tank

Police dog